YYUR
YYUB
ICUR
YY 4 ME!

yours till the banana splits!

Luv, Amelia Luv, Nadia

by Marissa Moss

(and two terrific letter-writers, Amelia and Nadia, best friends, together and apart)

D-LATER
D-LETTER
D-MADDER
I-GETTER

yours till the sun sets

UR 2 GOOD
2 B TRU

D-LIVER
D-LETTER
D-SOONER
D-BETTER

American Girl™

To Marje -
write back soon!

Pleasant Company
Publications
8400 Fairway Place
Middleton, Wisconsin 53562

letters and cards by Amelia, too → Book Design by Amelia ← Don't forget about Nadia!

Library of Congress Cataloging-in-Publication Data
Moss, Marissa.
Luv, Amelia luv, Nadia / by Marissa Moss.
p. cm.
Summary: Ten-year-old Amelia exchanges letters and postcards with her long-distance friend Nadia. Includes actual letters folded and inserted into envelopes.
ISBN 1-56247-839-7
ISBN 1-56247-823-0 (pbk.)
1. Toy and movable books Specimens. [1. Friendship Fiction. 2. Letters Fiction 3. Postcards Fiction 4. Toy and movable books.]
I. Title.
PZ7.M8535 Lu 1999
[Fic] --dc21
99-14222
CIP

First Pleasant Company Publications printing, 1999

Manufactured in Singapore
99 00 01 02 03 04 TWP 10 9 8 7 6 5 4 3 2

↖ Is this some strange zip code?

Nadia

me, Amelia

I've known Nadia since we started school together, and we've been best friends ever since. It's harder now that I've moved away, but we write letters and stay friends that way.

A letter from Nadia is like getting a visit from her.

cool handmade stationery

CAUTION CAUTION CAUTION CAUTION CAUTIO

Dear Amelia,

Remember when you wrote to me about the fire in your school? You said you felt better mailing your troubles away, but I felt bad that I couldn't do more for you.

Sometimes it's really hard to be a long-distance friend. Like I can't trick-or-treat with you this Halloween. I'll just have to mail you some candy, I guess. Maybe I could visit you during winter break. (I still haven't seen your new house!) But that's a long time to wait.

At school we're going to make a haunted house—it will be so ghoul! I wish you were here for it. I miss you.

luv, Nadia

U R 2 GOOD 2 B 4GOT 10!

food you always see in diners ↓

↑ grilled cheese with frilly toothpicks

crackers wrapped in crinkly cellophane— pull on the red tab to open

tuna melt— another frilly toothpick ↓

↑ (I got these postcards from D.D.'s Diner when we ate there last week. Mom said she was too tired to cook, which is always good news to me.) But now we can't eat out for a month because Mom got mad at Cleo for blowing her straw wrapper onto the back of a bald man's head.

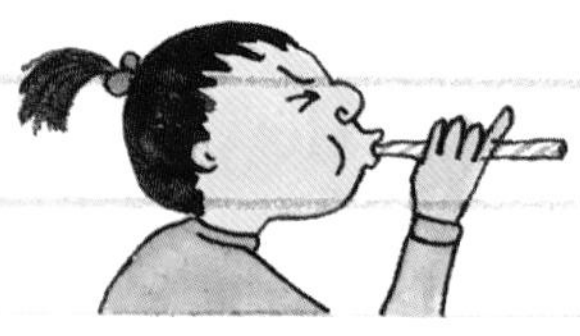

meat loaf— who goes to a restaurant and orders <u>this</u>?

ham and eggs— for breakfast, lunch or dinner

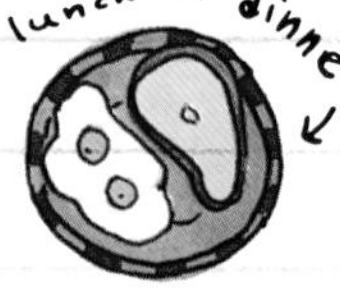

doughnuts in their own plastic case— DO NOT TOUCH!

D.D.'S DINER ←

getting a letter from you is like drinking hot chocolate out of a thick diner mug

Dear Nadia,

I miss you, too. And I wish I could help with the haunted house. My school isn't doing anything like that, but my teacher says maybe we'll have a pumpkin-carving contest— it's too early to decide yet. I hope we do. I want to make a Cleo jack-o'-lantern— <u>that</u> would be a veeeery scary face!

luv,
Amelia

yours till the tuna melts!

Nadia Kurz
61 South St.
Barton, CA
91010

more great postcards (maybe I'll be a postcard designer when I grow up — it looks like fun!)

Dear Nadia,

We went here on a field trip. It was great! I got lots of ideas for my notebook. I might even make my own comic book. Also, if I don't carve a Cleo jack-o'-lantern, I'll do a cartoony character, somebody I invent myself. Like Power Pumpkin — faster than a speeding zucchini, able to leap giant watermelons in a single bound, more powerful than a bulb of garlic!

Write back soon!

luv, Amelia

yours till the foot prints!

Nadia Kurz
61 South St.
Barton, CA
91010

prints from high heels — or exclamation points on their sides?

I got these comic book stamps at the museum, too. You can arrange them into your own comic strip.

Nadia still hasn't written back. Did my postcard have bad breath? Does my writing stink?

DELAYED MAIL SERVICE

I consulted Cleo's Magic 8 Ball—

"Will Nadia write back to me today?"

It said, "Ask again later." That's no answer!

unfinished letter business

Will I never learn more about Nadia's mysterious haunted house? What about her promise to send me candy? And she hasn't told me what her costume is going to be or asked about mine. She said she missed me!

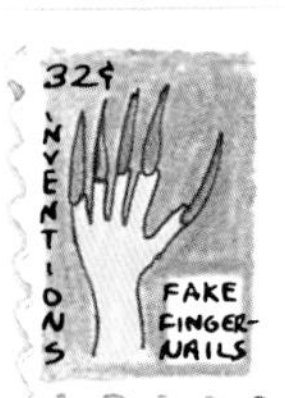

You know how in old movies they show time passing by pages being torn off a calendar? That's how I felt waiting for a letter from Nadia. Days passed, but the mailbox stayed empty.

still, I wrote to her — I'm faithful!

the enclosed card

Dear Amelia,

I haven't written because:
(check one)

- ☐ I have an awful wart on my finger that makes picking up a pen painful.
- ☐ I fell, hit my head, and now have amnesia.
- ☐ I already wrote to you a zillion times — the post office must have lost the letters.
- ☐ I'm writing to you right away — expect a letter <u>any</u> second!

Amelia
564 N. Homerest
Oopa, Oregon
97881

Yes!! Finally, finally, FINALLY, a letter from Nadia!

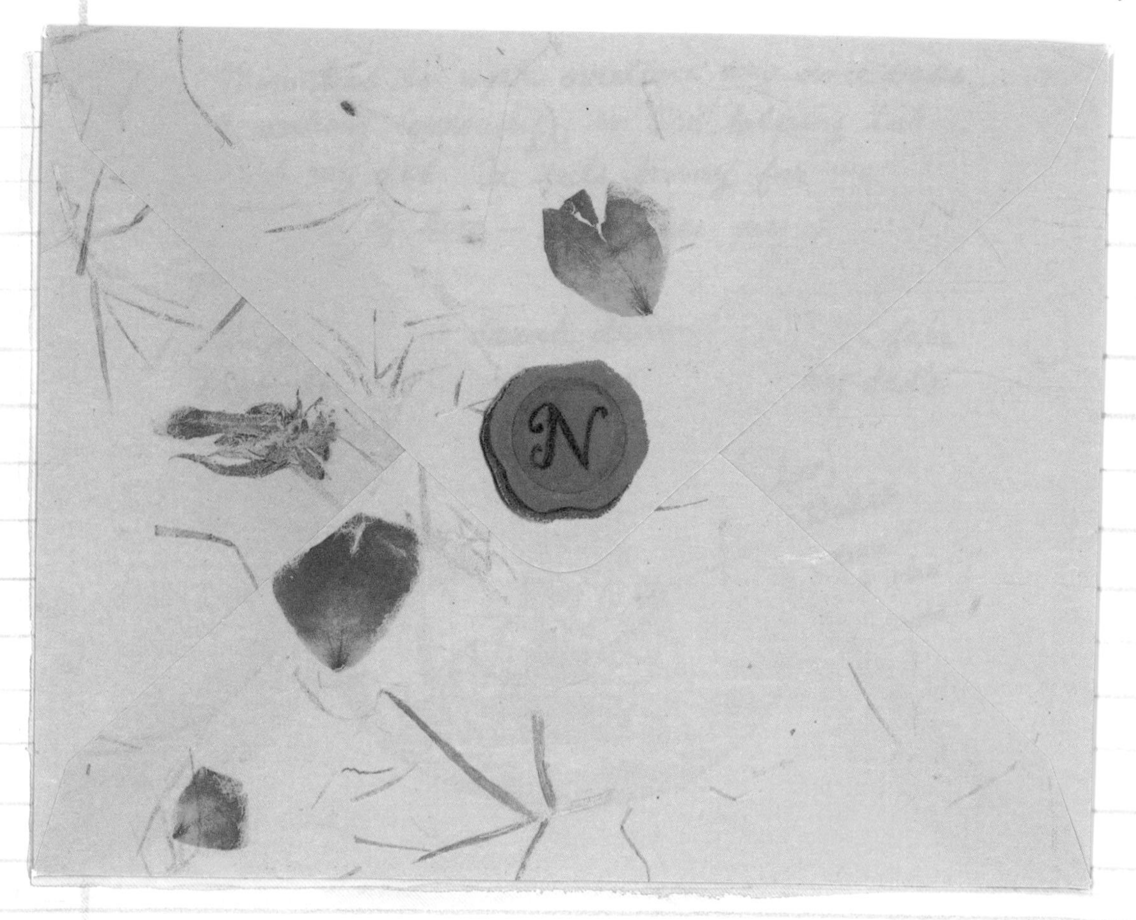

I was never mad at Nadia — well, maybe a little. Mostly I was worried (and I was right to be worried!).

I felt bad, badgering Nadia to write to me when she had all that stuff on her mind. I want to help her, not bug her.

GET-WELL HINTS (OR WHAT TO DO FOR SICK PEOPLE)

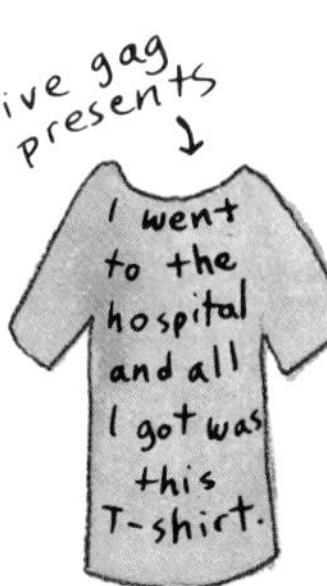

Dear Nadia,

That's horrible, what happened to your dad. I'm so sorry! I hope they take away the drunk's car. He should never drive again. I'm sending a get-well card to your dad, and my mom is sending flowers.

At least he's home from the hospital—hospitals are the worst. I hate the smell—part disinfectant, part cafeteria food.

It's funny, but your letter gave me an idea. Maybe that's what happened to my dad. Maybe he died in a car crash, and we never found out. My mom never talks about him. I asked Cleo, but she says she was 2 years old when he left so she doesn't remember him at all. He must have left right after I was born. Did he leave because of me? But I was such a cute baby.

If he was in a car crash, that would explain why he never writes to us.

luv, Amelia

yours till the first aids

or brand-new comic books

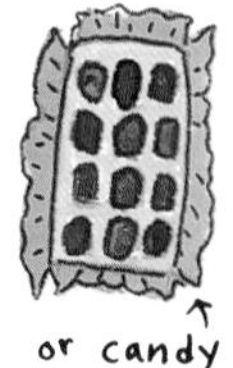

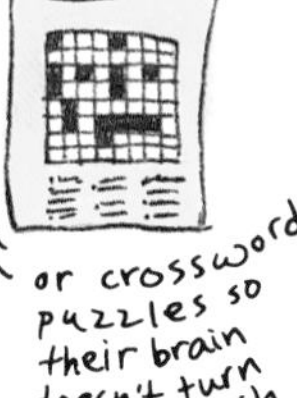

or food that tastes good.

This is how I imagine Nadia's dad.

The only good thing about a hospital is you can push a button to move your bed and watch TV all day.

This would be handy to have at home.

Amelia
564 North Homecrest
Oopa, Oregon
97881

This stationery looks like one of my notebook covers.

Dear Amelia,

It's strange to see my dad this way. I don't know how to explain it. He's still very weak and groggy from painkillers, so I help him eat and drink (like hold the glass up for him when he drinks through the straw). He makes jokes about it and calls me his "babysitter" (at least I don't have to change any diapers!).

I can tell he doesn't like having to ask me for help all the time, but I really don't mind. I just pretend I'm a nurse — in a way, I am. It makes me feel important. And I feel lucky. I can walk around while he's stuck in bed most of the time.

luv,
Nadia
yours till the ink blots

I try to imagine Nadia as a nurse, fluffing pillows and helping her dad.

Nurse Nadia (in those quiet, oh-so-white nurse shoes)

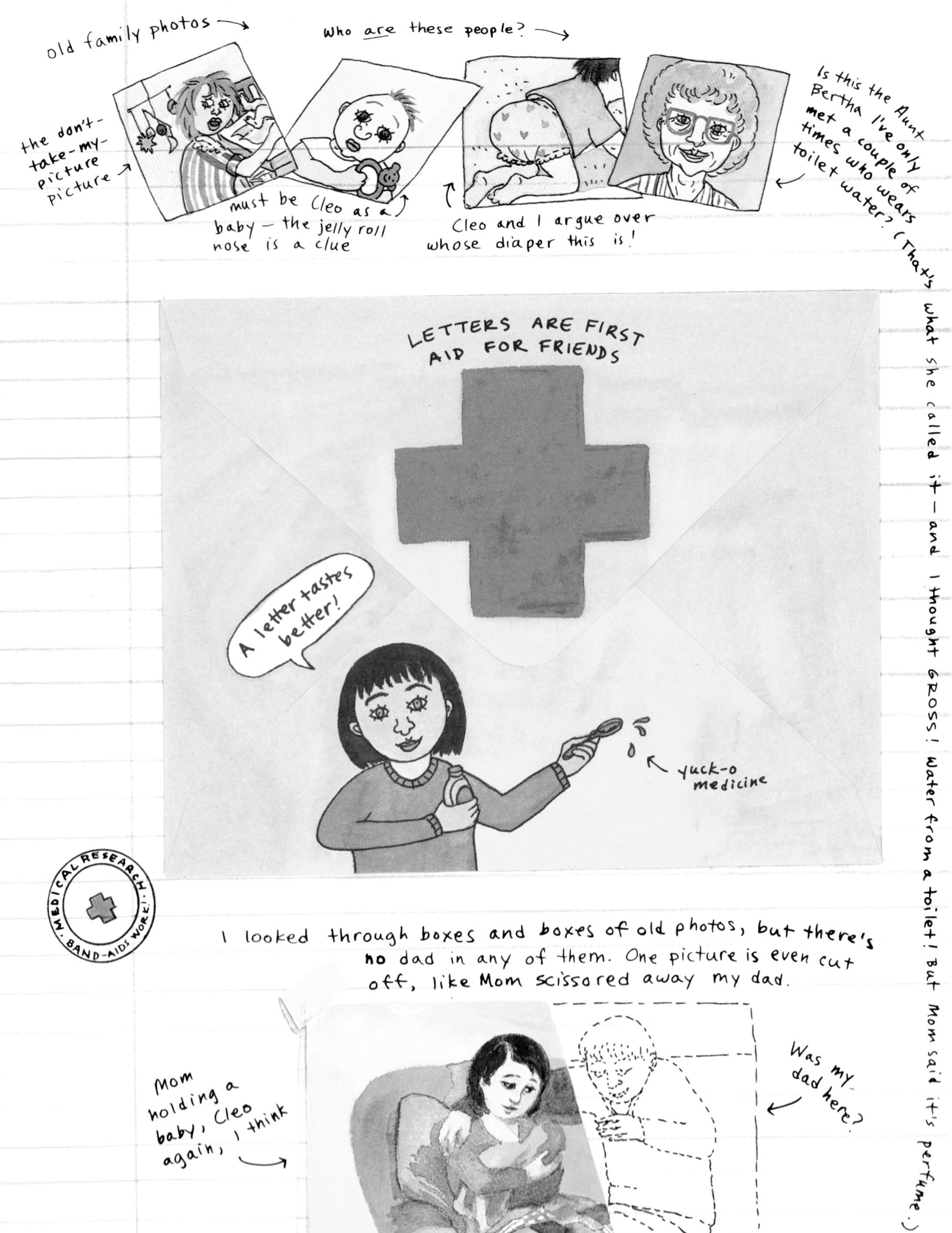

I looked through boxes and boxes of old photos, but there's no dad in any of them. One picture is even cut off, like Mom scissored away my dad.

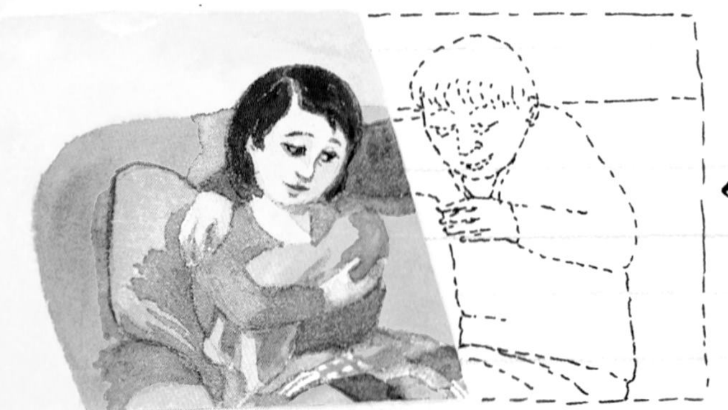

↙ Nadia's beginning to sound a little like a crabby grown-up.

I'M FEELING A BIT BUGGY!

Dear Amelia,

Yes, you have a right to know about your dad. You're reminding me that I'm lucky to _have_ a dad. Right now I need that.

At first it was kind of fun helping Dad. It made me feel grown-up. But now I'm not so sure. I mean, it's a _lot_ of _work_, and it's getting in the way of my regular life. Someone comes in to help him while I'm at school, but she leaves when I get home. Dad says he waits all day for me because I'm more fun than the helper. (I remember when _I_ used to wait for _him_ to come home!) It's nice he needs me, but it's also not nice. Do you know what I mean?

luv,
Nadia
yours till the horse flies
2 or not 2

things that make grown-ups grouchy →

↖ bad grades on tests

the sound of Saturday morning cartoons ↑

asking about dads who went away ↓

↙ socks left innocently on the floor

↖ anything spilled

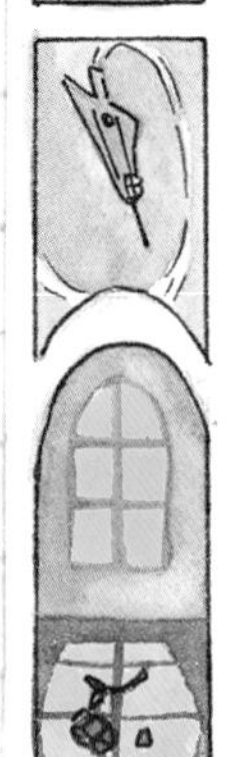

Dear Nadia,

I kind of know what you mean about your dad needing you. Moms and dads are supposed to be the grown-ups — not you! I can't imagine taking care of Mom that way. She never asks anyone for help. I did make tea for Cleo once when she was sick. Does that count?

Ever since the field trip to the comic art museum I've been making comic strips, so I'm sending you one. It's more work to make a cartoon than you might think!

Maybe my next comic strip will be about a girl detective searching for a mysterious man. (Is he her father?) luv, Amelia

yours till the comic strips

I made Nadia a comic strip to cheer her up.

PSSST! OPEN THIS ENVELOPE FOR A SURPRISE!

Dear Amelia,

Thanks for the comic strip. I love it! I wish I was Power Pumpkin — then I could leave my dad and go trick-or-treating. Mom asked the person who takes care of Dad during the day to come Halloween night (Mom has to work then). At first the helper said yes, but now she says no. So I'm stuck at home!

I wish I had a sister — even one like Cleo! Then this wouldn't all fall on me. Halloween only comes once a year, and I'm going to miss the whole thing.

I'm mad at Mom and mad at Dad, too. I know it's not his fault, but playing cards or Monopoly isn't the same as trick-or-treating.

luv, Nadia

yours till the jelly fishes

(P.S. Maybe I'll invent my own game of Monopoly — that's a way to have fun.)

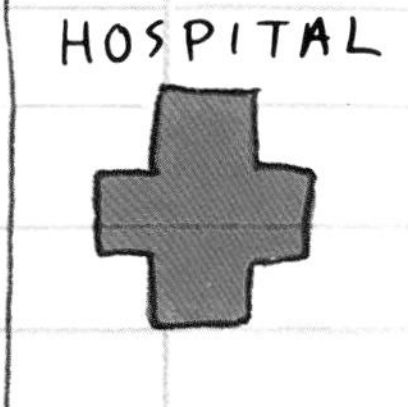

Don't land here!

Nadia needs a new chance.

OREGON | CALIFORNIA

why not these states for names?

I like the Scottie dog marker best.

How did they think of using an iron for a marker?

Dear Nadia,

I'm sorry about Halloween. Tell you what— I'll trade Cleo for your dad (since you're desperate for a sister). I know you're bored, but when you write about playing cards with your dad I wish I could, too (not with your dad, but with mine).

Everytime I see a strange man now (especially if he has a jelly roll nose!), I can't help but wonder, is that guy my dad? How about him over there?

I've searched everywhere for some clue about who he is — in all the old photos and boxes of junk Mom keeps. I found my old glow-in-the-dark yo-yo, but that was it. I feel like I'm haunted by a ghost dad — if I could put a face to that ghost it wouldn't bother me so much.

Speaking of ghosts, how's the haunted house going? At least that gives you some kind of Halloween. You can still have the fun of dressing up.

I haven't decided on a costume yet. I'm too distracted wondering if my dad is something great like a rocket scientist or something boring like an orthodontist.

luv, amelia

yours till the house paints

MANHOLE COVER DESIGNER

CHOCOLATE TASTER

WATCH MODEL

PUDDLE JUMPER

STORE WINDOW PAINTER

MASK MAKER

COOKIE BAKER

TELEGRAM SINGER

CAN STACKER

I'm trying to imagine spending too much time with my dad. Would it be like being stuck in the car on a long drive with carsick Cleo?

Dear Amelia,

I can't believe you'd want to be stuck like me. At least Mom is trying to find someone to stay with Dad on Halloween night. She's asked all her friends (now she jokes that she's asking her enemies). But you know what Halloween is like — everyone wants to be at a party or doing something fun.

Dad feels terrible for me. He even told me to just go trick-or-treating and leave him by himself. But how can I do that?

So now I'm trying to cheer him up about my missing Halloween. Pretty funny, huh?

At least I do have the haunted house. You're right — that counts for something.

luv,
Nadia
yours till the phone calls

(P.S. My bet is that your dad is a writer or artist.)

winding road — queasiness ahead

sharp turn — get ready to be thrown across the backseat

steep grade — prepare for jerky braking

help — we've run out of room for this road!

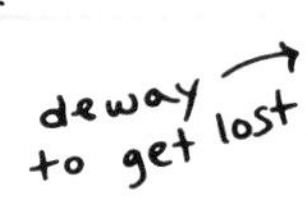

deway to get lost

games to play with stuck-at-home dads

card games

board (bored) games

WITCH'S BREW

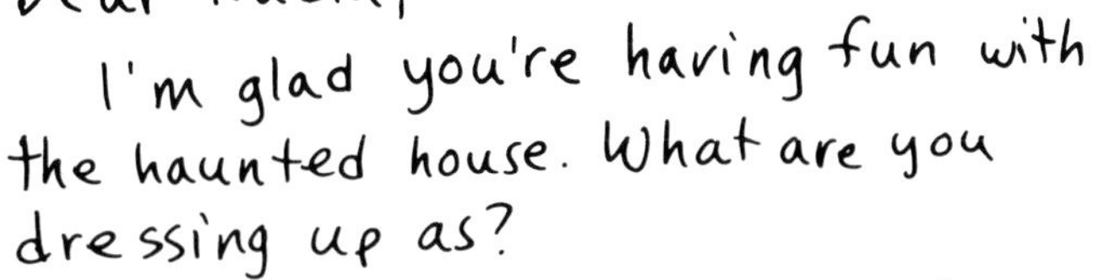

Dear Nadia,

I'm glad you're having fun with the haunted house. What are you dressing up as?

I'm still deciding on a costume. I was going to be a vampire, but I tried some of those plastic fangs and they were just too uncomfortable. (And they made me drool. Cleo said that made my vampire more realistic, but I don't care— if I wanted to drool, I'd go as a giant baby.)

drooly vampire

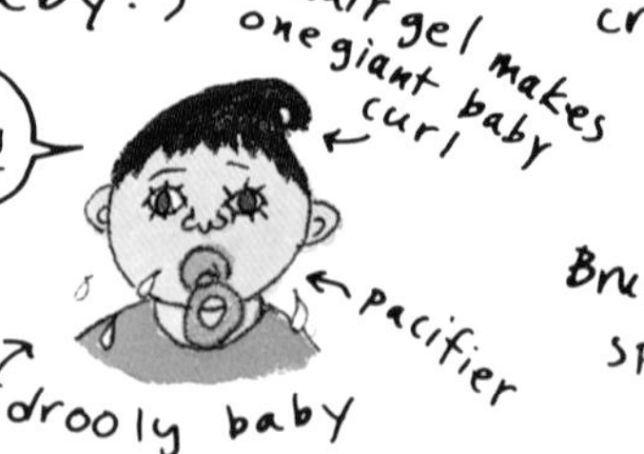

drooly baby

I even thought I'd dress up as my dad, but that would take too much imagination. (Besides, I don't have a dad to borrow a coat and tie from, so forget it.)

luv,
amelia

yours till the ice screams

(P.S. Maybe your dad will have a miracle recovery before Halloween. I'm keeping my fingers crossed!)

ingredients

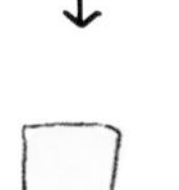

tofu

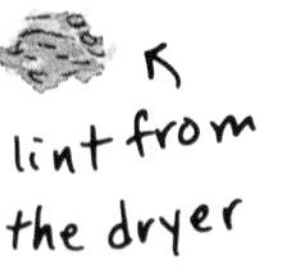

lint from the dryer

suspicious green specks you picked out of your casserole

runny eggs

rejected Halloween candy

nasty cough syrup

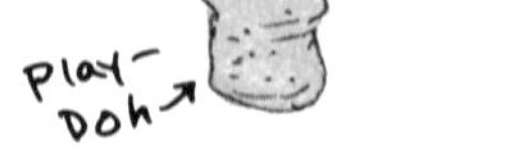

Play-Doh

mystery mush

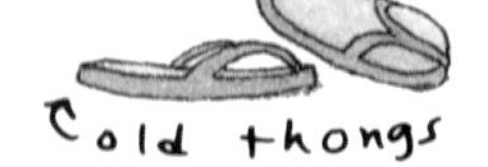

old thongs

ingredients

old shoelaces

toilet water—eeew!

stale sandwich crusts

Brussels sprouts

prunes

old Band-Aids

hangman

tic-tac-toe

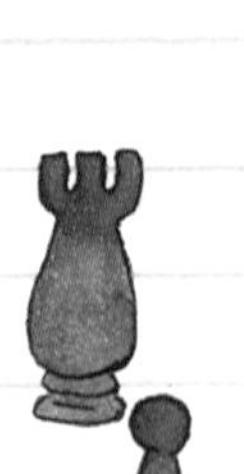

chess

games not to play with sick dads

Twister

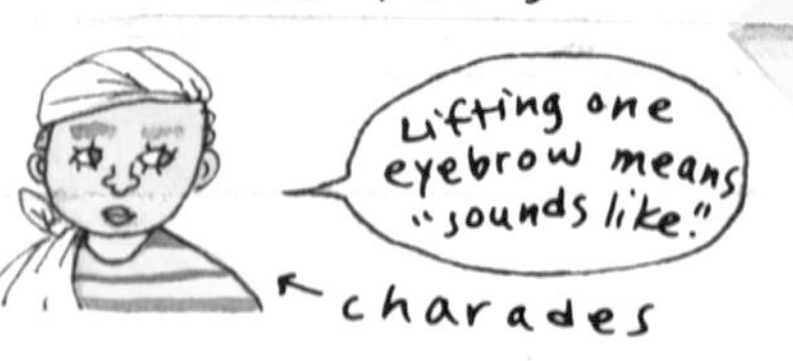

charades

Dear Amelia,

I'm not counting on a miracle recovery here. I'm just trying to figure out a way to have some fun on Halloween. I will get to be at the haunted house in the afternoon, but I don't know what my part is yet.

For the evening Dad wants to rent some corny old movie — like the original black-and-white Frankenstein. I'm trying to act like I love his idea, but I don't think I'm fooling anyone. I wish I was a bird — then I could just fly out the window and be free, free, free.

Dad's promised to have my favorite pizza delivered for dinner on Halloween. And Mom said that for once I'll be allowed to eat in front of the TV. Well, at least that's something.

luv,
Nadia

yours till the vampire bats!

haunted house features

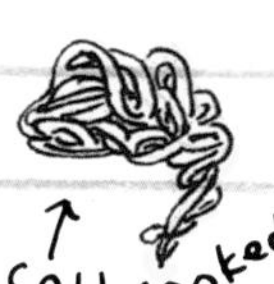

cold cooked spaghetti for intestines

peeled grapes for eyeballs

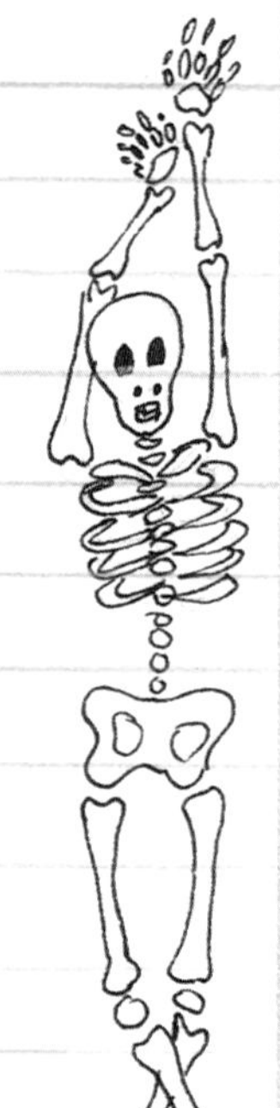

skeletons that jump out to scare you

BUMP

CLUMP

THUMP

heavy monster footsteps

sheets hanging up as ghosts — ooooh! I'm so scared!

joke gravestones

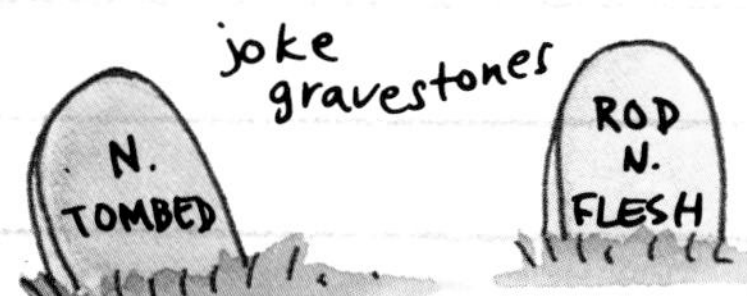

I. M.
DEAD

"Cleo" fits Cleo perfectly, no matter what her mood is.

happy

Gnaaak!

asleep

bored

wryly amused

fuming

guffawing

melodramatic

not listening to Mom

befuddled

terrified

meaning business

worried

Dear Nadia,

Guess what? I finally found out something about my dad! Mom didn't mean to talk about him, but Cleo was whining about her name, how strange it is, how no one else is ever named Cleo, and Mom got all huffy and said, "What's wrong with 'Cleo'? I love 'Cleo.' I argued so hard with your father for that name that he finally gave in. But then, of course, he insisted on naming Amelia."

My dad picked my name! He must have liked me after all. That shows he cared, doesn't it?

luv,
Amelia
yours till the name tags

(P.S. I wish I could spend Halloween with you, even if it means watching an old movie.)

Now that Cleo knows Mom named her after Cleopatra, Queen of the Nile, she's got an even bigger head.

I feel different about my name knowing my dad chose it. It's like a mysterious clue he left behind. How did he know Amelia would fit me so perfectly?

Was I named after Amelia Earhart, the pilot?

Is there some other famous Amelia I don't know about?

I'm trying to picture Nadia as a mummy, but all I can think of is my daddy. (If you cross a mummy with a daddy do you get a muddy or a dummy or a muddy dummy?)

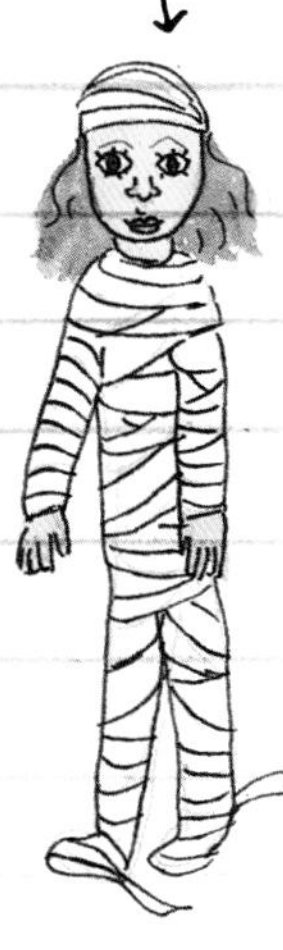

Dear Amelia,

The haunted house is finished, and now we're taking kids through it. My job is to be a mummy that leaps out and laughs maniacally (I mean, like a maniac). It's a lot of fun! But I can only stay an hour after school because Dad's helper will only stay that long. At least I have that hour!

The first day I worked, I brought Dad a little present to cheer him up. I've been so crabby even though I try hard not to be.

funny glasses like this—he loved them!

I like the story about your name. Dad said that Nadia was the only name he and Mom both liked.

luv, Nadia

yours till the broom sticks

← extra mummy wrappings

← witch with a turbo-charged broom

Cleo as the Queen of the Nile — all that makeup makes her more like a clown than a queen

Cleo's friend Gigi is going as a biker chick — she borrowed her brother's leather jacket and motorcycle helmet

she looks GREAT! Gigi always is cool no matter what she wears.

MATCH THE GLASSES TO THE FACES

Dear Nadia,

Your letter gave me a great idea! If you can't trick-or-treat, Halloween can still come to you. You've just got to dress up! Since your dad's all bandaged up and has casts on, why doesn't he be a mummy, just like you are for the haunted house? Wrap a bandage around his head and he'll really look the part! You two can be mummy twins and scare the trick-or-treaters when you give out candy.

I asked Mom why my dad named me Amelia. She said he'd always loved that name and he was a big fan of Amelia Earhart. I love the idea of being named after her! Maybe I'll be the first woman to do something, too — like go to Mars!

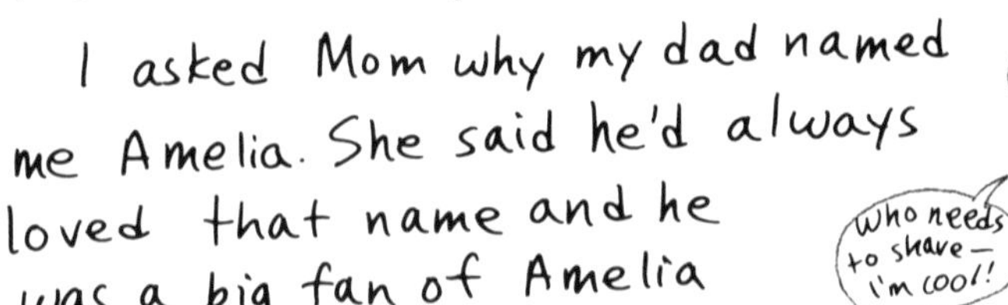

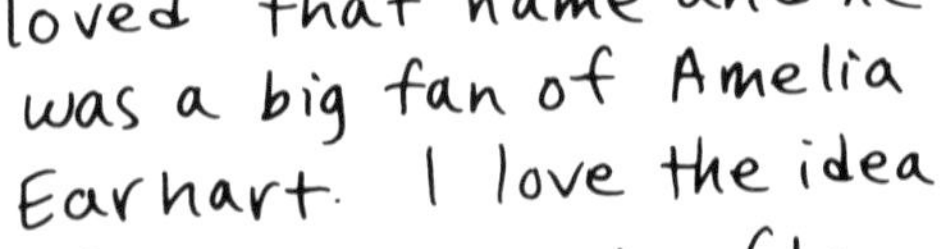

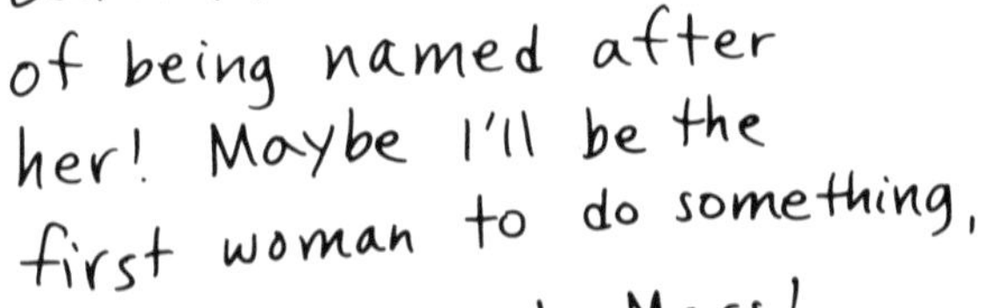

luv, amelia

Yours till the foot falls

Peace, man.

tie-dye hippie type

jowly old man type

Who needs to shave — I'm cool!

cool dude type

granny type

Hi, hon!

gum-chewing, bright red lipstick, big-hair type

Dear Amelia,

Dad loves your mummy idea and so do I! It's just what he needed to lift his spirits (get it — ghosts, spirits?). Now he's all excited about Halloween. Me, too! I'm even going to make a costume for myself — not a mummy (you'll see!).

One good idea deserves another, so here's one for you: Why don't you just ask your mom for your dad's address and tell her you won't bug her anymore, you'll bug him instead. I bet she says yes. Why not? (I mean, why is she still so mad at him? They've been apart a long time now.)

luv,
Nadia
yours till the finger nails

healthy "treats" you don't want to get for trick-or-treating ↓

↗ a box of raisins

↑ a pencil

worst of all — a toothbrush!

THINGS YOU NEED A FRIEND FOR

Dear Nadia,

Thank you, thank you,

THANK YOU!

You were right! Mom's so sick of my nagging, she gave me Dad's name and address and said to just leave her alone. His name is Quentin. Quentin?! And he lives in Chicago. Now that I have his address, I'm not sure what to write to him. I want him to write back, so I've got to be careful what I say.

If I tell him anything about Cleo, I definitely won't ever hear from him. Part of me is worried I will hear from him — and I won't like him. What if he's disappointed with me or I'm disappointed with him?

luv, Amelia

yours till the card tricks

Dear Amelia,

Good luck with your dad. I bet he'll write back to you. Just tell him about yourself.

We're all set for Halloween now! Everyone's costume is ready (Mom's a witch like she is every year—only this year she'll wear her costume to work!), and the yard looks creepy, as it should. I still wish I could trick-or-treat, but I haven't forgotten about sending you candy—in my next letter.

luv, Nadia yours till the pitch forks!

I imagine my dad doesn't wear glasses or have a jelly roll nose. →

← I think he has a friendly face.

modern art jack-o'-lanterns ↓

traditional ↓

MUSEUM OF COMIC ART — SHAZAM!

Dear Nadia,
I still haven't written to my dad yet, but I've been busy making my costume. And yesterday was the pumpkin-carving contest. There were some really good jack-o'-lanterns. I was going to make a Cleo face, but at the last minute I changed my mind and carved a face like I imagine my dad's looks like. I made myself a pumpkin dad! (I know his skin isn't really orange, but it was cool to have his face in front of me, even in the form of a jack-o'-lantern!) luv, amelia

yours till the face masks

MASQUERADE

12¢

Nadia Kurz
61 South St.
Barton, CA
91010

fancy ↓

jack-o'-lantern snowman ↓

I still have postcards from the Comic Museum.

headless jack-o'-lantern ↓

family of jack-o'-lanterns →

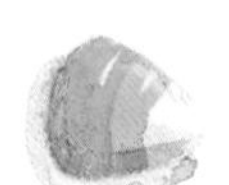

gummy worms

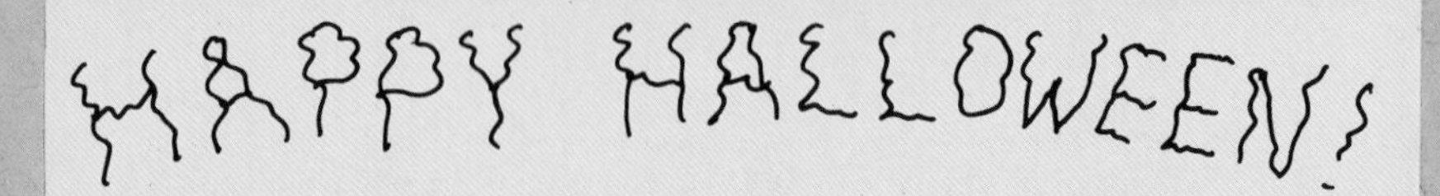

Guess what! I was giving out candy with Dad (he had a great time, thanks to you) when the doorbell rang and it was a big witch - Mom! She came home earlier after all so I could go trick-or-treating. It was great! (And good thing I'd made a costume like you'd suggested - I was ready to go!) I even gave Dad all his favorite candies - we were both happy!

Here's my Halloween costume - a crayon!

I can't draw, but you get the idea.

luv, Nadia

yours till the pencil points

Nadia sent candy like she said she would - very sweet of her. I'm so glad she got to trick-or-treat after all.

old-people candy that kids never eat

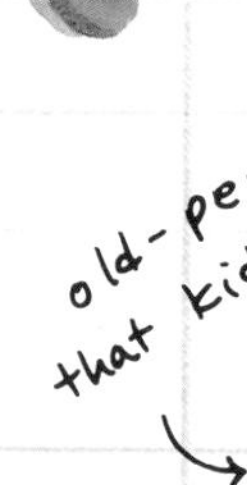

gross flavor like prune or coffee-cherry or pineapple-toffee

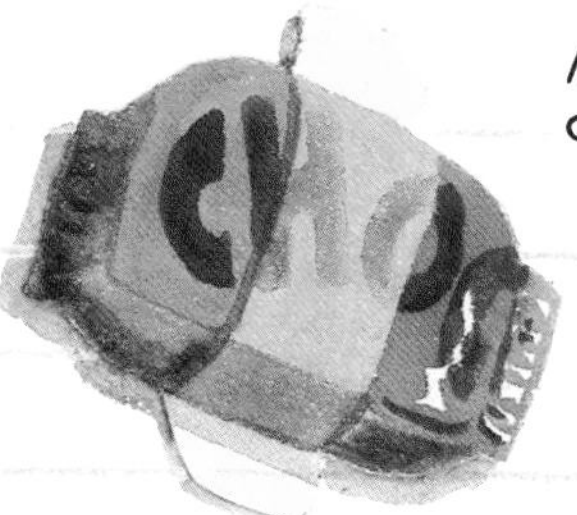

little candy bar

gum-yum!

Even living far apart, Nadia and I still think alike — we even made costumes that went together!

When we were little we always made costumes that went together.

Amelia
564 North Homerest
Oopa, Oregon 97881

EXTREMELY URGENT!

In old movies, the important news is always delivered in a telegram. They didn't have any punctuation so they used the word "stop" instead of periods. Sounds funny!

NADIAGRAM · TELEGRAM · NADIAGRAM
(OR AN OLD-FASHIONED KIND OF FAX)

GREAT NEWS STOP DADS CASTS ARE OFF STOP HE IS BACK AT WORK STOP BUT HE SAYS WE CAN STILL PLAY CARDS STOP WE WONT STOP STOP AND I WONT STOP WRITING LETTERS EITHER STOP WRITE BACK SOON STOP DONT YOU EVER STOP STOP LUV NADIA STOP YOURS TILL THE BUS STOPS STOP

Nadia Kurz
61 South St.
Barton, CA 91010

RADIOACTIVE TELEGRAM: OPEN AT ONCE TO PREVENT THERMONUCLEAR DISASTER!

When I lived near Nadia, we could talk with tin-can telephones. Now we use telegrams!

CONGRATULATIONS STOP

DO YOU HAVE TIME NOW TO VISIT ME STOP YOU CAN STOP BY STOP I WOULD LOVE TO SEE YOU STOP OUR FRIENDSHIP WILL NEVER STOP STOP LUV AMELIA STOP YOURS TILL THE SHORT STOPS STOP a very happy envelope, like at the end of a story

more happy endings

dog wagging its tail

the last drop of hot chocolate

the end of a sappy movie

Dear Amelia,

Mom and Dad say that maybe for winter break I can visit you. (I've earned it!!) But for now I have a great idea. I'm sending you back all the letters and cards you sent (not the candy–I ate that!) so you can put them in a scrapbook together with the letters I sent you. That way we'll have a kind of letter-story about when my dad got hurt, and you discovered your own dad.

chirp! chirp!

luv, Nadia
yours till the rain bows

(P.S. Do you like this idea?)

     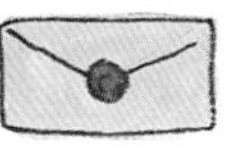

Dear Nadia,

I LOVE your idea. I've started the scrapbook already. I'm saving the last page for something we'll write together when you come. That seems like a good ending for a letter story.

Mom says life's not like books with tidy endings. But sometimes you can make a happy ending — like we are!

I want to make a happy ending with my dad, too. I'm thinking of sending him a comic strip because sometimes I think better in pictures than in words. You have a dad, you know how to talk to him — do you think it's a good idea?

Anyway, I hope this will be a beginning, not an ending at all. We'll see...

luv, Amelia

yours till the moon beams

more happy endings

pumpkin pie for dessert

the last day of school

the space shuttle lands successfully

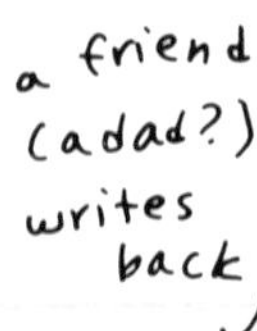

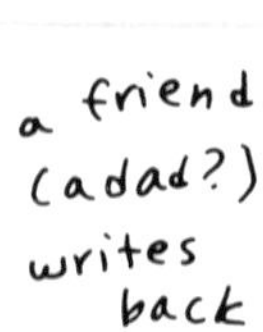

a friend (a dad?) writes back

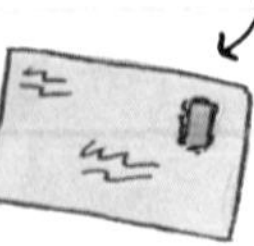

When Nadia got my last letter, she called and we had a long talk about dads (she's a real expert now!). And she said to send the comic strip, so here goes nothing — I'm mailing it today!

another happy ending — little man sweeping up the end of the cartoon

This scrapbook is proof that you can stay friends even when you live far away from each other. You just have to write, write, write!

I wonder if that means you can become friends even if you live far apart as long as you write, write, write? Can I write my way into knowing my dad? I started this scrapbook waiting for an answer to a letter and now I'm waiting again!

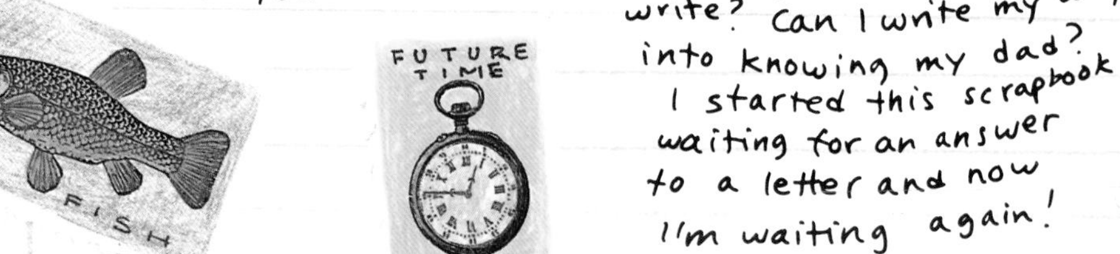